T0399034

First published in Great Britain 2025 by Farshore
An imprint of HarperCollins*Publishers*
1 London Bridge Street, London SE1 9GF
www.farshore.co.uk

HarperCollins*Publishers*
Macken House, 39/40 Mayor Street Upper,
Dublin 1, Ireland, D01 C9W8

ISBN 978 0 00 868760 1
Printed in the United Kingdom
1

A CIP catalogue record for this book is available from the British Library.

	MIX
	Paper | Supporting responsible forestry
FSC www.fsc.org	FSC™ C007454

This book contains FSC™ certified paper and other controlled
sources to ensure responsible forest management.

For more information visit: www.harpercollins.co.uk/green

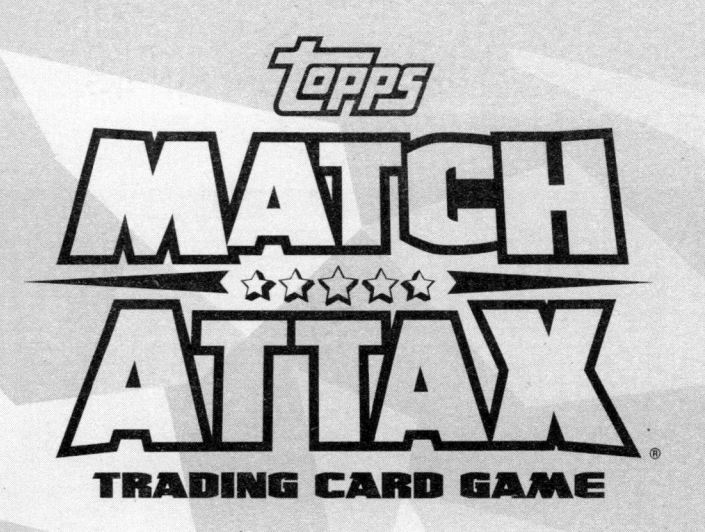

ALL-NEW

MEGA

TRIVIA

WELCOME TO

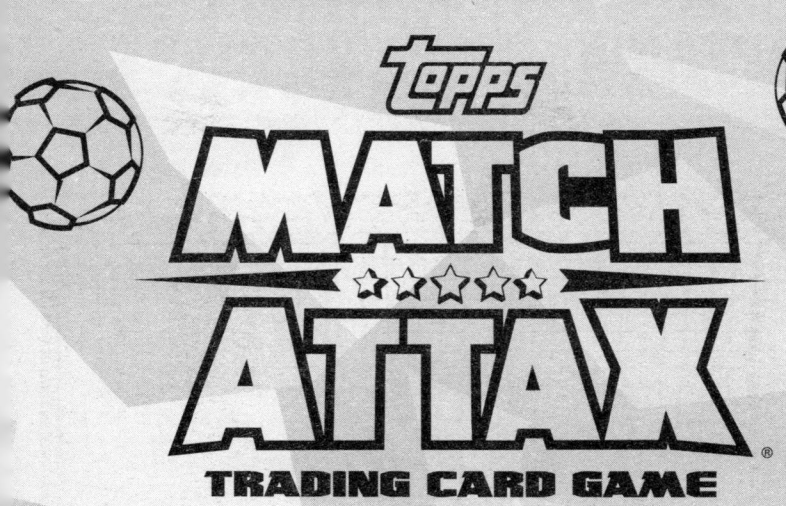

topps MATCH ATTAX
TRADING CARD GAME

ALL-NEW
MEGA TRIVIA

Get ready to learn the secrets behind every position on the pitch and discover what gives the game's superstars the edge over their opponents!

This **EPIC** book is bursting with **FOOTY FACTS**, **SUPER STATS**, **AWESOME PUZZLES** and **COOL QUIZZES** all about the exciting world of **FOOTBALL**!

ARE YOU READY FOR KICK OFF?

COOL CAPTAINS

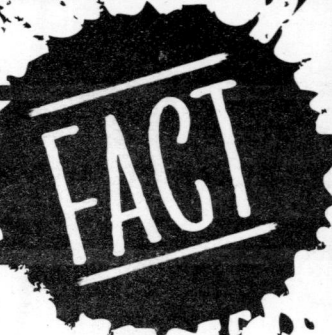

FACT

Every team needs a leader on the pitch. It's the captain's duty to communicate and inspire the team, and guide them through the good times and the bad. It's a mega responsibility!

SKILL 1
GOOD COMMUNICATOR
Most captains are natural leaders and will take responsibility on the pitch. If there's a problem, they're first on the scene!

SKILL 2
REFEREE RESPECT
Captains are the only players that can talk to the referee. They must treat the match officials with maximum respect and pass on any important messages to their teammates.

SKILL 3
CLUB DUTY
Whilst the captain guides the team during a match, they must also set an example at the training ground and represent the club throughout the local community.

VIRGIL VAN DIJK

A rock in the heart of Liverpool's defence, van Dijk is cool under pressure and inspires Liverpool's dominance!

LIVERPOOL

LAUTARO MARTÍNEZ

Martínez led Inter Milan to the Italian top-flight title with his energetic forward play and eye for goal. His team know he'll always perform!

INTER MILAN

KYLE WALKER

With years of experience at the top level, Kyle has seen it all. He keeps a cool head and leads City from defence to attack.

MANCHESTER CITY

⟩ STARTING LINEUP

There's a big match coming up and you need to create an ultimate squad to lift the trophy! Can you complete a team of 11 to make an epic starting lineup?

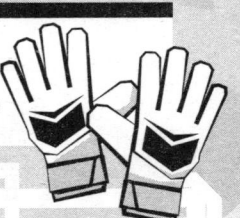

GK

RB   **CB**   **LB**

CM   **CM**

RW   **LW**

RF   **CF**   **LF**

DREAM TEAM MANAGER'S NAME

DIFFICULTY: ⚽⚽

TRUE ≫ OR ≪ FALSE?
EPIC EDITION!

1

Manchester City are known by their fans as the Blues With Wings.

TRUE ☐
FALSE ☐

2

The 2024 UEFA European Championships final was played at Olympiastadion, Berlin.

TRUE ☐
FALSE ☐

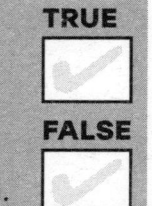

3

Until the 2005-06 season, all English top-flight matches were played on Wednesdays.

TRUE ☐
FALSE ☐

In 2023-24, Manchester United Women won a major cup final by four goals over Tottenham!

TRUE ☑

FALSE ☑

VAR is used in all English top-flight matches. It stands for Video Assistant Referee.

TRUE ☑

FALSE ☑

In the 2020-21 season, Crystal Palace scored an incredible 314 goals in 38 matches.

TRUE ☑

FALSE ☑

From the 2025-26 season, match officials will wear white shirts, white shorts and green socks.

TRUE ☑

FALSE ☑

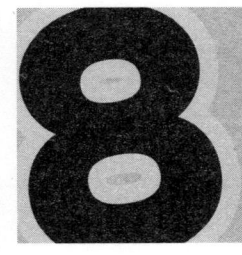

Real Madrid won a historical league and UEFA Champions League double in the 2023-24 season.

TRUE ☑

FALSE ☑

Answers on page 81

GOALKEEPERS

Goalkeepers are the last line of defence when it comes to keeping a clean sheet for the team. How well do you know the world of great saves?

1 Which of these goalkeepers is the captain of their club?

- [ ] Ederson
- [ ] Alphonse Areola
- [ ] Manuel Neuer
- [ ] Nick Pope

2 Who kept six clean sheets in the 2023-24 UEFA Champions League?

- [ ] Gregor Kobel
- [ ] Yann Sommer
- [ ] Jan Oblak
- [ ] Alphonse Areola

3 Which 'keeper lifted the league title with Bayer Leverkusen in 2023-24?

- [ ] Kevin Trapp
- [ ] Thibaut Courtois
- [ ] Sam Johnstone
- [ ] Lukas Hradecky

4 In English top-flight history, who has achieved the most clean sheets?

- [ ] Petr Čech
- [ ] Jordan Pickford
- [ ] Emiliano Martínez
- [ ] Aaron Ramsdale

5 Legendary goalkeeper Mary Earps made her full England debut in which year?

- [x] 2011
- [ ] 2017
- [x] 2021
- [x] 2022

6 Yvon Mvogo made the most saves in the 2023-24 French top-flight league. Which team does he play for?

- [ ] FC Lorient
- [x] Nice
- [ ] Marseille
- [x] Monaco

7 In the 2023-24 Scottish top-flight league, how many clean sheets did Rangers' Jack Butland keep?

- [ ] 8
- [x] 10
- [ ] 18
- [ ] 2

8 In the 2023-24 English top-flight season, which goalkeeper conceded the most goals?

- [x] Thomas Kaminski
- [ ] Guglielmo Vicario
- [x] Alisson Becker
- [x] Wes Foderingham

9 Belgian Maarten Vandevoordt is the youngest ever goalkeeper to play in the UEFA Champions League. How old was he at the time?

- [x] 21
- [x] 24
- [x] 11
- [x] 17

10 Which squad number is traditionally used by a club's goalkeeper?

- [ ] 99
- [x] 20
- [x] 1
- [x] 11

Answers on page 81

MATCH ATTAX MIX-UP

DIFFICULTY: ⚽

This Match Attax card has been divided into six strips. Your task is to put the card back together. Can you work out what order the strips need to go in?

A	B	C	D	E	F

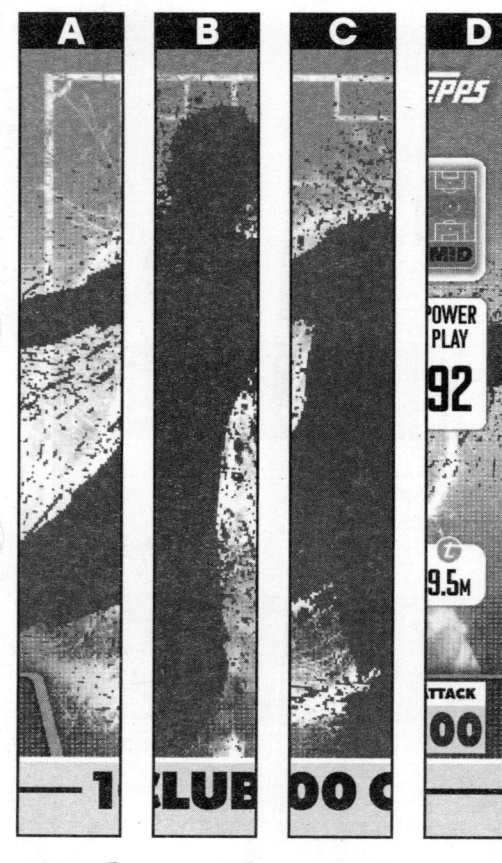

JUDE BELLINGHAM REAL MADRID

POWER PLAY
92

9.5M

ATTACK
00

DEFENCE
82

1	2	3	4	5	6
?	?	?	?	?	?

DIFFICULTY: ⚽

Like a defender trying to track a speedy forward, you'll need to pay close attention to these lines. Only one of them makes it to the goal – can you work out which?

START

A B C D E F G

NO GOAL

NO GOAL

NO GOAL

NO GOAL

NO GOAL

NO GOAL

ANSWER ___

GOAL!

 **MYSTERY STARS 1**

These world-famous players are keeping their identity top secret! Read the clues for each player then have a go at guessing who they really are.

PLAYER 1

I play for Manchester City and was top scorer in the 2023-24 women's top-flight league!

PLAYER 2

I'm a striker for Aston Villa, but I also provide my team with loads of assists!

PLAYER 3

My goals helped Chelsea win the English women's top-flight league in 2023-24!

PLAYER 4

I've played in goal for 10 years for Spanish giants, Barcelona!

BALL DESIGNER

CREATE!

Every European competition and top-flight league has its own ball design. Grab some pens and unleash your creativity by designing one of your own!

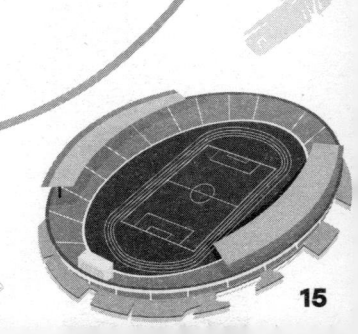

ENGLISH WOMEN'S LEAGUE

The English women's top-flight league has some of the best players in the world and enjoys record-breaking attendances!

DIFFICULTY: ⚽⚽

1 Chelsea won the English women's top-flight league in 2023-24. Including that win, how many times have they won in a row?

- [ ] 5
- [ ] 13
- [ ] 26
- [ ] 1

2 How many hat-tricks has Vivianne Miedema scored in the league?

- [ ] 2
- [ ] 3
- [ ] 4
- [ ] 5

3 Which team plays all of their home matches in a blue kit?

- [ ] Liverpool
- [ ] Arsenal
- [ ] Leicester
- [ ] West Ham

4 In the 2022-23 season, how many matches did Chelsea win out of 22?

- [ ] 13
- [ ] 19
- [ ] 15
- [ ] 21

5 What nationality is Tottenham Hotspurs' Bethany England?

- [ ] German
- [ ] Scottish
- [ ] Welsh
- [ ] English

6 Which team did Fran Kirby play for before Brighton?

- [x] Arsenal
- [x] Everton
- [x] Chelsea
- [x] Aston Villa

7 In the 2014 season, what was the winning margin at the top of the league table?

- [x] 0 points
- [x] 1 point
- [x] 8 points
- [x] 12 points

8 Sophie Ingle has the most English women's top-flight league appearances in history. How many matches has she played?

- [x] Over 180
- [x] Over 350
- [x] Over 450
- [x] Over 600

9 Which club play some of their home matches at Emirates Stadium?

- [x] West Ham
- [x] Arsenal
- [x] Liverpool
- [x] Everton

10 Which of these players has never won the Golden Boot trophy?

- [x] Rachel Daly
- [x] Sam Kerr
- [x] Mary Earps
- [x] Khadija Shaw

Answers on page 82

GOALKEEPER GREATS

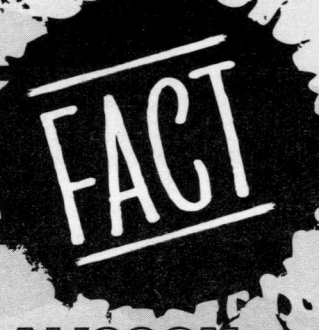

Strength, positioning and acrobatic agility are all important skills for the best goalkeepers in the game! Let's take a look at the secrets behind this important position!

SKILL 1
AWESOME AGILITY
A goalkeeper needs to move quickly. From patrolling the penalty area to diving between their posts, they must be ready to jump around!

SKILL 2
STAY FOCUSED
There can be long periods of the game when the ball doesn't come near the goal. A top 'keeper can stay focused and be ready to perform at a split-second's notice!

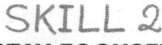

SKILL 3
PLAY FROM THE BACK
A modern goalkeeper is often tasked with turning defence into attack. They must be comfortable passing to their defenders or looking for long balls forward.

ALISSON BECKER

Alisson has won almost every cup! He's known for solid positioning and one-on-one domination!

LIVERPOOL

GREGOR KOBEL

Kobel has been in the team of the season for the past two years. He's the only Swiss 'keeper to play in a UEFA Champions League final. Legend!

BORUSSIA DORTMUND

JAN OBLAK

Superstar Oblak signed for Atlético ten years ago and is one of the world's best. He's tall and agile, making him a monster shot stopper!

ATLÉTICO MADRID

BALL COUNTING

You're in goal for a training drill and the entire team are taking shots! How many balls can you count in this hectic shooting scene?

THERE ARE ___ BALLS.

CHAMPIONS LEAGUE

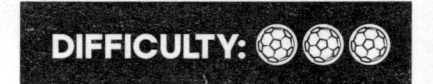

It's official: the UEFA Champions League is the greatest club competition in Europe! How well do you know the top teams and awesome action?

1 Which team has won the most UEFA Champions League titles, with 15?

- [ ] Arsenal
- [ ] Real Madrid
- [ ] Real Betis
- [ ] Barcelona

2 Who were the competition's two top scorers in the 2023-24 season?

- [ ] Erling Haaland
- [ ] Karim Benzema
- [ ] Harry Kane
- [ ] Kylian Mbappé

3 How many teams were in the 2023-24 season group stages?

- [ ] 64
- [ ] 12
- [ ] 32
- [ ] 20

4 Who's played the most minutes in UEFA Champions League history?

- [ ] Lionel Messi
- [ ] Iker Casillas
- [ ] Sergio Ramos
- [ ] Lautaro Martínez

5 How many different clubs have won the UEFA Champions League?

- [ ] 44
- [ ] 2
- [ ] 32
- [ ] 23

6 How many times has manager Carlo Ancelotti won the UEFA Champions League?

- [ ] 7
- [ ] 5
- [ ] 3
- [ ] 12

7 How many times was Sergio Ramos sent off whilst playing for Real Madrid in the tournament?

- [ ] 4
- [ ] 2
- [ ] 3
- [ ] 13

8 Which superstar has scored the most goals in UEFA Champions League history, with 141 goals?

- [ ] Cristiano Ronaldo
- [ ] Son Heung-min
- [ ] Jude Bellingham
- [ ] Callum Wilson

9 The fastest goal in UEFA Champions League history was scored after how many seconds?

- [ ] 10.1
- [ ] 1.3
- [ ] 22.6
- [ ] 13.2

10 Which stadium has never hosted a UEFA Champions League final?

- [ ] Wembley
- [ ] Estádio da Luz
- [ ] San Siro
- [ ] Turf Moor

Every club has its legends – the players that achieved greatness by giving everything on the pitch whether they lost, drew or won. Can you draw a line between the legends and their clubs?

LEGEND

CLUB

LEGEND	CLUB
SERGIO AGÜERO	BAYERN MUNICH
SAM KERR	BARCELONA
FRANCESCO TOTTI	MANCHESTER CITY
ZINÉDINE ZIDANE	CHELSEA
WAYNE ROONEY	LIVERPOOL
MANUEL NEUER	ROMA
AITANA BONMATÍ	REAL MADRID
STEVEN GERRARD	MANCHESTER UNITED

CUP FINAL SCORERS

Every player dreams of scoring a goal in a final! From domestic cups to the UEFA Champions League, players can write their names in the history books! Read the clues and try to complete the crossword.

DOWN

2 _ _ _ _ _ _ Putellas scored in the 95th minute to confirm the 2023-24 UEFA Women's Champions League win for Barcelona (6)

4 Cristiano _ _ _ _ _ _ _ has scored more goals in UEFA Champions League finals than any other player, with four (7)

6 The last goal in the 2023-24 UEFA Champions League final was scored by _ _ _ _ _ _ _ _ Júnior (8)

8 The 2023-24 UEFA Europa League final was won thanks to a hat-trick by Atalanta's Ademola _ _ _ _ _ _ _ (7)

ACROSS

1 Midfield magician _ _ _ _ _ scored Manchester City's winning goal in the 2022-23 UEFA Champions League final (5)

3 _ _ _ _ Williams scored Spain's first goal in the 2024 European Championships final (4)

5 A major 2024 cup final was won by Manchester Utd thanks to a goal from Kobbie _ _ _ _ _ _ (6)

7 In the 2022-23 Europa Conference League final, Jarrod _ _ _ _ _ scored West Ham's winning goal (5)

ENGLISH LEAGUE

Known as one of the greatest divisions in the world, the English top-flight league is full of superstars and incredible stats!

DIFFICULTY: ⚽ ⚽ ⚽

1. Which club has won the current English top-flight league more than any other in history?

- [ ] Manchester Utd
- [ ] Chelsea
- [ ] Arsenal
- [ ] Liverpool

2. Who does Spanish goalkeeper David Raya play for?

- [ ] West Ham
- [ ] Aston Villa
- [ ] Arsenal
- [ ] Brentford

3. Which player made the most passes in the 2023-24 season?

- [ ] Bukayo Saka
- [ ] Willian
- [ ] Alex Iwobi
- [ ] Rodri

4. Which team received the most red cards (7) in the 2023-24 season?

- [ ] Burnley
- [ ] Chelsea
- [ ] Luton
- [ ] Arsenal

5. In 2024-25 how many top-flight league teams are based in London?

- [ ] 2
- [ ] 4
- [ ] 10
- [ ] 7

6

Which English top-flight club's stadium has the smallest capacity?

- [ ] Bournemouth
- [ ] Aston Villa
- [ ] Southampton
- [ ] Leicester

7

In the 2024-25 season, how many clubs have a stadium capacity of over 60,000 seats?

- [ ] 2
- [ ] 5
- [ ] 9
- [ ] 13

8

In the current English top-flight league's history, which club has scored the most goals from headers?

- [ ] West Ham
- [ ] Liverpool
- [ ] Luton
- [ ] West Brom

9

Thomas Frank is the manager of which top-flight team?

- [ ] Chelsea
- [ ] Fulham
- [ ] Newcastle
- [ ] Brentford

10

Who was the league's top scorer in the 2023-24 season?

- [ ] Erling Haaland
- [ ] Cole Palmer
- [ ] Phil Foden
- [ ] Ollie Watkins

Answers on page 84

>> DREAM DEFENDERS

Defenders are the base of any successful team. A strong defence provides a solid foundation that keeps their goal safe and operates as an outlet to the rest of the team!

SKILL 1
READING THE GAME
The game's great defenders are always watching the action unfold. They react to everything, making sure they are in the best position!

SKILL 2
COOL AND COMBATIVE
Defenders often get into physical battles with opposition attackers. They need to keep their cool and be professional – or they'll be in trouble with the ref!

SKILL 3
TACKLING TECHNIQUE
Stretching for a last-gasp tackle can result in stopping a goal ... or a disastrous foul. Developing good technique is important for any defender!

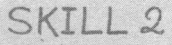

DAVID ALABA
Versatile Alaba can play anywhere across defence and has a slick left foot to move the ball forward!

REAL MADRID

WILLIAM SALIBA
Saliba's arrival in Arsenal's first team has coincided with their title-challenging form. He's a leader, with pace, agility and a mean tackle!

ARSENAL

KIM MIN-JAE
Tall, strong and fast, Kim often breaks up opposition moves and retains the ball to start his own team's attacks. He can really control a match!

BAYERN MUNICH

KIT DESIGN

Your club gets a new kit every season. Will this be the one that sees them win a trophy or lift a cup? Design your team a new kit to wear as they write their name in the history books!

CREATE!

TRUE ≫ OR ≪ FALSE?

CORNER CAPERS!

1

In the 2023-24 English top-flight season, James Ward-Prowse scored directly from a corner kick!

TRUE ☑

FALSE ☑

2

In a 2020-21 Spanish top-flight league match, an amazing 769 corner kicks were taken.

TRUE ☑

FALSE ☑

3

In the history of the English top-flight league, only once has a goalkeeper taken a corner kick!

TRUE ☑

FALSE ☑

 Corners are awarded if the ball comes off the defence, and crosses the line either side of the goal.

TRUE ☑

FALSE ☑

 The 2011-12 German top-flight league title was won by Borussia Dortmund with a goal directly from a corner.

TRUE ☑

FALSE ☑

 When a corner is being taken, opposition players must be at least 10 yards from the corner.

TRUE ☑

FALSE ☑

 In the English top-flight, James Ward-Prowse has taken more corners than any other player.

TRUE ☑

FALSE ☑

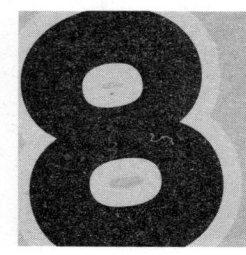 Players are only allowed to take a corner with the weaker of their two feet!

TRUE ☑

FALSE ☑

Answers on page 84

MIGHTY MANAGERS

DIFFICULTY: ⚽⚽⚽

A manager can transform the fortunes of a club. It's the most important job in football – they're responsible for picking the team and choosing the tactics for every match!

1. Which manager has won the top-flight league in five countries?

- [ ] Carlo Ancelotti
- [ ] Gary O'Neil
- [ ] Erik ten Hag
- [ ] Xabi Alonso

2. Mikel Arteta has transformed which club into title challengers?

- [ ] Sevilla
- [ ] Manchester City
- [ ] Arsenal
- [ ] Tottenham

3. Who led Manchester United to a league and cup treble in 1998-99?

- [ ] Roberto Mancini
- [ ] Mark Hughes
- [ ] Thomas Tuchel
- [ ] Sir Alex Ferguson

4. Which club did Xabi Alonso lead to an unbeaten domestic season?

- [ ] Bayer Leverkusen
- [ ] Bayern Munich
- [ ] Liverpool
- [ ] Borussia Dortmund

5 Which manager gave himself the nickname, 'The Special One'?

- [ ] Pep Guardiola
- [ ] Arne Slot
- [ ] José Mourinho
- [ ] Ange Postecoglou

6 How old was Roy Hodgson when he became the oldest manager ever in the English top-flight league?

- [x] 65
- [ ] 54
- [x] 101
- [x] 76

7 How many points did Brendan Rodgers' Celtic score in their record 2016-17 Scottish top-flight season?

- [ ] 106
- [ ] 95
- [ ] 91
- [ ] 86

8 With 2.34 points won per match, who's statistically the best manager in English top-flight history?

- [ ] Pep Guardiola
- [ ] Jürgen Klopp
- [ ] José Mourinho
- [ ] Russell Martin

9 In the 2022-23 English top-flight, a record number of managers were sacked. How many were replaced?

- [ ] 11
- [ ] 14
- [ ] 19
- [ ] 20

10 Who managed Paris Saint-Germain to the 2023-24 French league title?

- [ ] Luis Enrique
- [ ] Unai Emery
- [ ] Xabi Alonso
- [ ] Mauricio Pochettino

CODE BREAKER

The coach has scribbled a tactical message for their team. Using the code-breaking instructions in the box below, work out what the message is!

3 8 1 14 7 5 20 15 20 8 5
14 5 23 6 15 18 13 1 20 9 15 14
23 5 16 18 1 3 20 9 3 5 4!

CODE BREAKING RULES

Each number represents where the letter comes in the alphabet. For example, 1 is A, 18 is R and 26 is Z.

THE CODED MESSAGE IS:

_ _ _ _ _ _ _ _ _ _ _

_ _ _ _ _ _ _ _ _ _ _ _

_ _ _ _ _ _ _ _ _!

MYSTERY STARS 2

We've found more world-famous players keeping their identity a total secret! Read the clues for each player and have a go at guessing who these mystery stars really are.

PLAYER 1

I was voted as the Spanish top-flight's player of the season, and scored loads!

PLAYER 2

I'm a super defender who left Lille to sign for Manchester United in the summer of 2024!

PLAYER 3

After years scoring for fun in Paris, I'm now loving playing as a forward for Real Madrid!

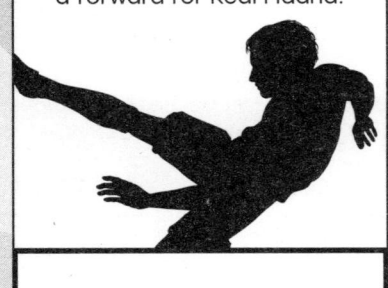

PLAYER 4

I play in midfield for Barcelona and in 2023 I won the Ballon d'Or Féminin!

GERMAN LEAGUE

The fiercest rivalries in world football and two of the biggest club stadiums in Europe? Welcome to the German top-flight league!

DIFFICULTY: ⚽ ⚽ ⚽

1 What is the seating capacity for Borussia Dortmund's stadium, Signal Iduna Park?

- ☑ 69,102
- ☑ 81,365
- ☑ 100,209
- ☑ 20,000

2 Which goalkeeper was named in the 2023-24 team of the season?

- ☑ Gregor Kobel
- ☑ Fabian Bredlow
- ☑ Manuel Neuer
- ☑ Kevin Trapp

3 The lowest capacity stadium in the division belongs to which club?

- ☑ Mainz 05
- ☑ Freiburg
- ☑ Wolfsburg
- ☑ Heidenheim

4 How many German top-flight titles have Bayern Munich won?

- ☑ 33
- ☑ 56
- ☑ 19
- ☑ 7

5 Who was the league's top scorer in the 2023-24 season?

- ☑ Harry Kane
- ☑ Loïs Openda
- ☑ Serhou Guirassy
- ☑ Victor Boniface

6 Which club plays their home matches at the Red Bull Arena?

- [x] Köln
- [x] RB Leipzig
- [x] Mainz 05
- [x] Freiburg

7 How many clean sheets did Bayer Leverkusen's Lukas Hradecky keep in the 2023-24 season?

- [x] 1
- [ ] 7
- [x] 9
- [ ] 15

8 Alphonso Davies hit the highest speed in the 2023-24 season. How many kilometres per hour did he reach?

- [x] 36.41
- [x] 88.00
- [x] 15.73
- [x] 11.17

9 Which team scored the fewest penalties (1) in the 2023-24 season?

- [x] RB Leipzig
- [x] Mainz 05
- [x] Augsburg
- [x] Stuttgart

10 Who notched the most goal assists in the 2023-24 season?

- [x] Alejandro Grimaldo
- [x] Thomas Müller
- [x] Julian Brandt
- [x] David Raum

NEXT GEN STARS

FACT

The fans have been talking. There's a wonderkid coming through the ranks who will soon make it into the first team! Let's take a look at what it takes to become a star of tomorrow!

SKILL 1
TRAIN HARD
Even the most talented young players won't become a professional unless they work hard. They need to earn their place on any team!

SKILL 2
ALWAYS IMPROVING
If a young player makes it to the first team, their journey is only beginning. They need to improve and learn as much as possible from the experienced players around them.

SKILL 3
PICK YOUR POSITION
Decide on your preferred position early on and then get to work perfecting it. Watch the pros, practice every day and prove you can be trusted to deliver!

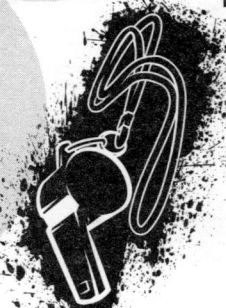

LAMINE YAMAL
Lamine became the youngest player to feature in a UEFA Euro Championship in 2024 ... and he scored!

BARCELONA

JÉRÉMY DOKU
Supersonic speed and tricky dribbling make Doku a defender's nightmare. He's already one of City's star players and the sky is the limit!

MANCHESTER CITY

JAMAL MUSIALA
Jamal is already a regular for Bayern and the German national team, thanks to his versatility and strength all across the pitch!

BAYERN MUNICH

NUMBER KNOWLEDGE

DIFFICULTY: ⚽ ⚽ ⚽

Every player on the team has an assigned squad number that they wear on the back of their shirt. Some players achieve huge success and are forever linked to their number! Can you write the numbers belonging to these famous players?

GROUP 1

MAC ALLISTER
SANÉ
GREALISH
BUENDÍA

GROUP 2

VINÍCIUS JR
GRIEZMANN
SAKA
TOONE

GROUP 3

SALAH
MARTINELLI
RAPHINHA
DOKU

FORWARD MEGA QUIZ

DIFFICULTY:

There's nothing like the thrill of your team scoring a goal – it's what football is all about! Take this quiz to see how well you know the greatest forwards in the game!

1 Who scored the most league goals in the 2023-24 English top-flight?

- Bukayo Saka
- Erling Haaland
- Alexander Isak
- Jarrod Bowen

2 Which Liverpool forward hit the woodwork most in 2023-24?

- Mohamed Salah
- Diogo Jota
- Darwin Núñez
- Luis Díaz

3 Who was the top scorer in the 2023-24 Spanish top-flight league?

- Álvaro Morata
- Jude Bellingham
- Artem Dovbyk
- Ante Budimir

4 In the 2023-24 Champions League, who had the most shots on target?

- Kylian Mbappé
- Raphinha
- Harry Kane
- Phil Foden

5 In the Women's Champions League 2023-24, who was the top scorer?

- [ ] Caroline Hansen
- [ ] Sam Kerr
- [ ] Aitana Bonmatí
- [ ] Kadidiatou Diani

6 Lautaro Martínez led Inter Milan to the Italian top-flight title in 2023-24! How many goals did he score?

- [ ] 24
- [ ] 14
- [ ] 4
- [ ] 34

7 How many goals did Harry Kane score as he took the German top-flight league by storm in 2023-24?

- [ ] 16
- [ ] 6
- [ ] 36
- [ ] 26

8 Which player scored two hat-tricks in 11 days during the 2023-24 English top-flight season?

- [ ] Dominic Solanke
- [ ] Ollie Watkins
- [ ] Son Heung-min
- [ ] Cole Palmer

9 Hearts' Lawrence Shankland was the Scottish league's top scorer in 2023-24, with how many goals?

- [ ] 12
- [ ] 2
- [ ] 24
- [ ] 32

10 Who assisted the most goals for their team in the 2023-24 season?

- [ ] Robert Lewandowski
- [ ] Mikel Oyarzabal
- [ ] Álex Baena
- [ ] Kylian Mbappé

SCOUT SEARCH

DIFFICULTY: ⚽⚽

Every club has a team of scouts that search the world for the best players. Can you find all the stars in the wordsearch below? Time yourself and tick them off as you discover them!

D	M	A	R	T	Í	N	E	Z	J
J	G	W	C	W	Z	I	E	O	I
S	A	J	M	E	M	S	U	L	P
A	V	H	U	I	N	A	Q	G	A
K	I	K	S	C	S	K	M	C	L
A	G	U	I	R	A	S	S	Y	M
Y	A	M	A	L	L	R	Z	F	E
Q	B	J	L	E	I	Q	R	K	R
Q	L	D	A	W	B	F	R	P	O
Z	U	J	V	T	A	C	I	Q	X
Z	X	B	O	W	E	N	S	K	L

FIND THESE

- ☑ GAVI
- ☑ GUIRASSY
- ☑ YAMAL
- ☑ ISAK
- ☑ BOWEN
- ☑ PALMER
- ☑ MUSIALA
- ☑ SAKA
- ☑ SALIBA
- ☑ MARTÍNEZ

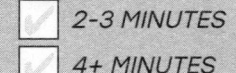

IT TOOK ME...

- ☑ UNDER 2 MINUTES
- ☑ 2-3 MINUTES
- ☑ 3-4 MINUTES
- ☑ 4+ MINUTES

THE BEST CLUB NICKNAMES

DIFFICULTY: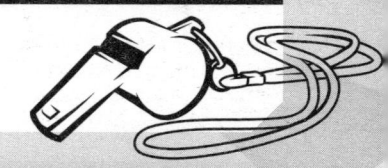

The match is underway and the crowd are roaring ... but who do they support? Draw a line between the clubs and their nicknames!

CLUB

- BAYERN MUNICH
- ASTON VILLA
- MANCHESTER CITY
- RB LEIPZIG
- ARSENAL
- RANGERS
- REAL MADRID
- MANCHESTER UNITED

NICKNAME

- THE GUNNERS
- THE RED DEVILS
- DIE ROTEN
- LOS BLANCOS
- DIE ROTEN BULLEN
- THE VILLANS
- THE CITIZENS
- THE GERS

Answers on page 87

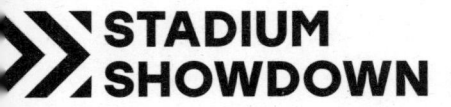
STADIUM SHOWDOWN

Every club has a home stadium where their fans watch them play. Some are old, many are new, but all of them are loved. Can you work out which stadiums are being described below?

STADIUM 1

The home of Real Madrid, this epic stadium can seat an incredible 80,000 fans!

STADIUM 2

The Reds' iconic stadium contains the Kop – a stand that can seat 12,850 fans!

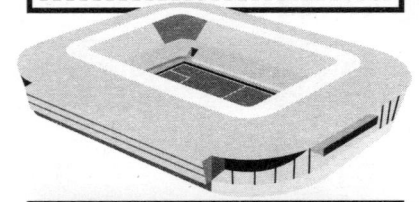

STADIUM 3

This stadium is nicknamed Paradise and is home to the club nicknamed The Bhoys!

STADIUM 4

Marseille's stadium is famous for its steep stands making their fans sound louder!

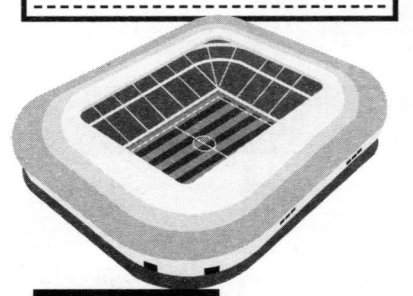

CREST CREATOR

You'll find a club crest on every professional football kit. It's an emblem that shows something special about the team. Design your favourite club a new one below!

SPANISH LEAGUE

The Spanish top-flight league is watched around the world. It has passionate fans and huge clubs – how well do you know it?

1 No club has won the Spanish top-flight league more than Real Madrid! How many times have they lifted the trophy?

- ☑ 51
- ☑ 22
- ☑ 36
- ☑ 40

2 Who were awarded the most penalties (9) in the 2023-24 season?

- ☑ Valencia
- ☑ Getafe
- ☑ Granada
- ☑ Almería

3 Which club shares the city of Madrid with two other teams?

- ☑ Girona
- ☑ Mallorca
- ☑ Espanyol
- ☑ Rayo Vallecano

4 Of these top-flight clubs, which is situated furthest west in Spain?

- ☑ Barcelona
- ☑ Real Madrid
- ☑ Osasuna
- ☑ Celta Vigo

5 What is the correct name of Barcelona's iconic home stadium?

- ☑ New Camp
- ☑ Nu Kampen
- ☑ Camp Nou
- ☑ Castle Camp

6 What is the Spanish word for the referee?

- [x] Árbitro
- [x] Rey
- [x] Ruffi
- [x] Maestro

7 In the 2023-24 season, Chimy Ávila received three red cards. Who does he play for?

- [x] Real Betis
- [x] Barcelona
- [x] Alavés
- [x] Espanyol

8 Which Las Palmas player made the most passes of anyone in the 2023-24 Spanish top-flight season?

- [x] Manu Fuster
- [x] Iván Cédric
- [x] Marvin Park
- [x] Kirian Rodríguez

9 How old was Lamine Yamal when he became the league's youngest ever scorer?

- [x] 16
- [x] 20
- [x] 19
- [x] 21

10 Which legendary player is the league's all-time top scorer?

- [x] Cristiano Ronaldo
- [x] Lionel Messi
- [x] Robert Lewandowski
- [x] Álvaro Morata

FOOTY FORMATIONS 1

We've seen some incredible formations before, but what's going on here? Draw pictures in the grids so that each column, row and box contains only one of each football symbol.

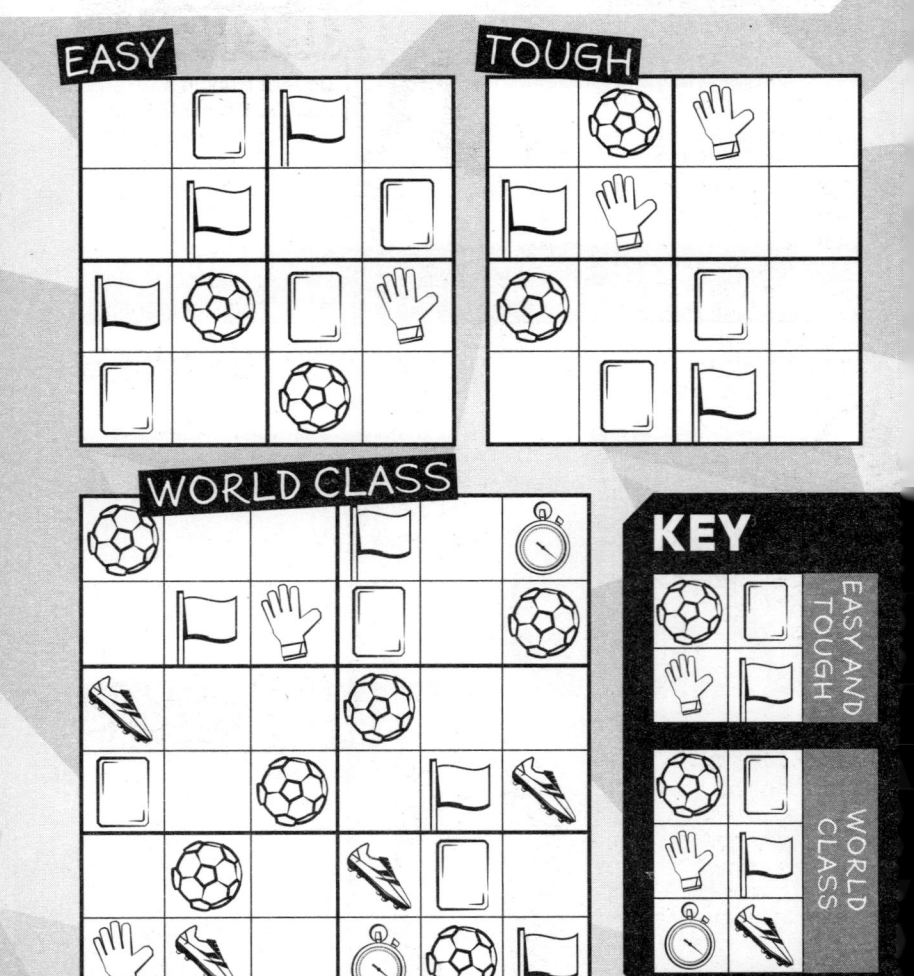

EASY

TOUGH

WORLD CLASS

KEY

EASY AND TOUGH

WORLD CLASS

MIDFIELD MASTERS

They rarely take the glory but holding midfielders are one of the most important positions on any football pitch. In every great team, there is a reliable marshal at the base of midfield.

SKILL 1

BREAK IT UP

Defensive midfielders use their high energy levels to close down the opposition and win back the ball. This makes it difficult for opponents to hold possession and build pressure.

SKILL 2

KEEP IT MOVING

Whether they're taking short passes from defenders or launching long balls forward, holding midfielders need to be ready to receive the ball and move it into space at a moment's notice.

SKILL 3

WHAT'S GOING ON?

Reading the game is a core skill in this position. The very best players know when to cover their defenders, how to crowd the midfield and when they are safe to make a surging run forward!

JOSHUA KIMMICH

Bayern Munich's Joshua Kimmich is an intelligent player, who is a solid defender and a gifted attacker. He's always looking for the ball!

BAYERN MUNICH

RODRI

Rodri is strong and tall, which makes him a powerful midfielder. He tackles well and is unbeatable in the air. His tactical mind brings calm to City!

MANCHESTER CITY

DECLAN RICE

No one carries the ball better than this Arsenal hero. With his athleticism and tough tackling, he is one of the best midfielders in world football!

ARSENAL

DIFFICULTY: ⚽ ⚽

TRUE
» OR «
FALSE?
CLUB KITS!

1
Atlético Madrid wear red and white stripes after using some Southampton kits in 1909!

TRUE ✓

FALSE ✓

2
Aston Villa were the first English league team to wear the famous claret and blue colours.

TRUE ✓

FALSE ✓

3
Paris Saint-Germain wore a kit the same colour as the Eiffel Tower until the 2016 season.

TRUE ✓

FALSE ✓

Real Madrid's iconic white shirts were inspired by a field of white grass located in Madrid.

TRUE ✓

FALSE ✓

Inter Milan and AC Milan used to wear all black kits, before adding their own coloured stripes!

TRUE ✓

FALSE ✓

Chelsea chose to wear blue kits after they were given the nickname 'The Blues'.

TRUE ✓

FALSE ✓

Celtic are famous for green and white hoops, but have played in all-green shirts before!

TRUE ✓

FALSE ✓

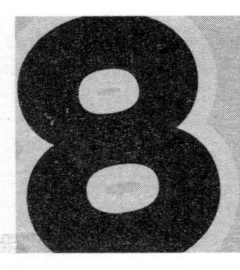

Newcastle United wore red home shirts, before switching to their famous black and white stripes.

TRUE ✓

FALSE ✓

Answers on page 89

STADIUM MEGA QUIZ

From local Sunday league sidelines, to the biggest stadiums in the world – football stadiums are places where magic is made! How well do you know Europe's greatest arenas?

1 The highest attendance for an English league match was Tottenham vs Arsenal with 83,222. Which stadium was it at?

- [ ] Wembley
- [ ] Anfield
- [ ] Old Trafford
- [ ] St. Mary's

2 After renovations, what will be the capacity of Barcelona's Camp Nou?

- [ ] 105,000
- [ ] 99,999
- [ ] 85,000
- [ ] 200,000

3 Chelsea's Stamford Bridge stadium first opened in which year?

- [ ] 1900
- [ ] 1901
- [ ] 2001
- [ ] 1877

4 Which club plays in the Italian top-flight league's newest arena?

- [ ] Cagliari
- [ ] Juventus
- [ ] Fiorentina
- [ ] Monza

5 With 67,394 seats, which club plays at the Stade Vélodrome?

- [ ] Lille
- [ ] Marseille
- [ ] Lens
- [ ] Nice

6 West Ham's London Stadium was built to host which sport?

- [ ] Rugby
- [ ] Athletics
- [ ] Mini golf
- [ ] Darts

7 What is the correct name of Fulham's riverside stadium?

- [ ] Riverview
- [ ] The Dome
- [ ] Full 'o' Fans
- [ ] Craven Cottage

8 Which Spanish top-flight team's stadium isn't on mainland Spain?

- [ ] Osasuna
- [ ] Sevilla
- [ ] Mallorca
- [ ] Valencia

9 Ibrox stadium is the home of which famous footy team?

- [ ] Rangers
- [ ] Nantes
- [ ] Celtic
- [ ] Bournemouth

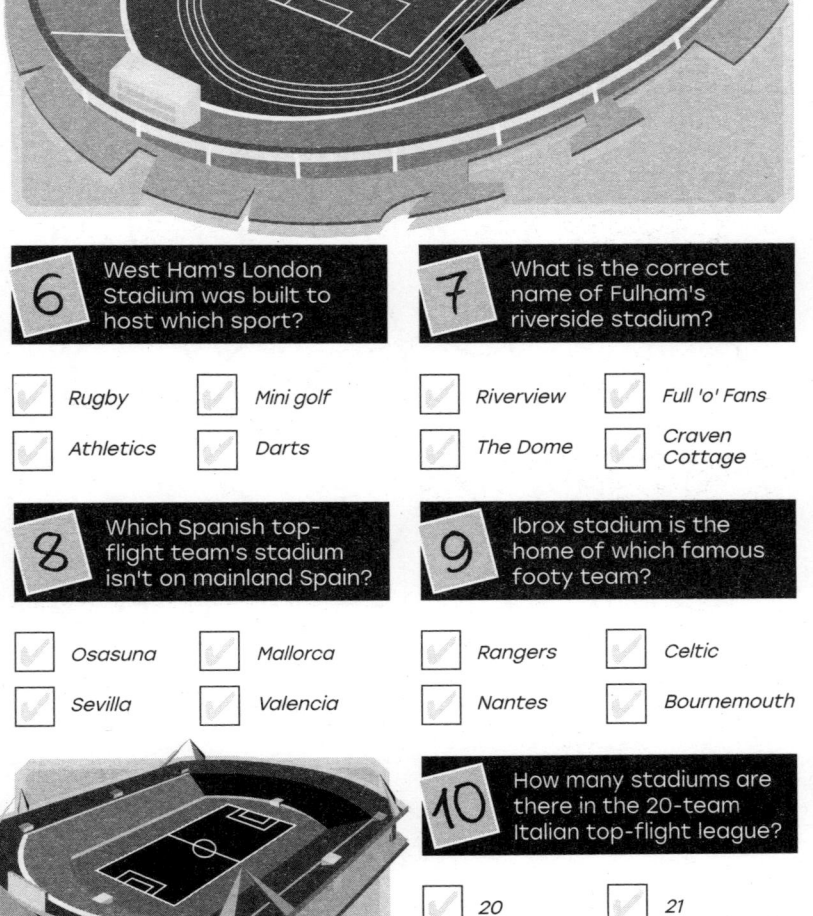

10 How many stadiums are there in the 20-team Italian top-flight league?

- [ ] 20
- [ ] 18
- [ ] 21
- [ ] 12

Answers on page 89

DREAM BOOTS

Boots you are comfortable in can give you the confidence to pass with precision and boss a match. Can you find the correct path to this pair?

ANSWER ___

MYSTERY STARS 3

DIFFICULTY:  ⚽⚽⚽

Can you work out who these world-famous players are? Read the clues and then try to guess the identity of each of these footballers.

PLAYER 1

I'm the 'Starboy' in London, where I celebrate goals by sitting on advertising boards!

PLAYER 2

I lifted the 2023-24 Women's Champions League trophy as captain of Barcelona!

PLAYER 3

I'm the only player to win the Best FIFA Women's Player award two years in a row!

PLAYER 4

In my first season at Real Madrid, I won the Spanish league's player of the season!

Answers on page 90

>> ACE ATTACKERS

Every position is important, but chances often turn into goals thanks to the finishing of a team's forward line. Let's take a look at what goes into being a fantastic foward!

SKILL 1
POSITIVE PRESSURE
Strikers are the first line of defence. They need to do a lot of running, closing down opposition players and breaking up play!

SKILL 2
INTELLIGENT MOVEMENT
Whether they're making runs between defenders, or finding a yard of space in the box, the best forwards make clever runs look simple!

SKILL 3
CLINICAL FINISHING
Forwards need to be ready to receive the ball at any moment. The best players must be able to finish with their left foot, right foot or head!

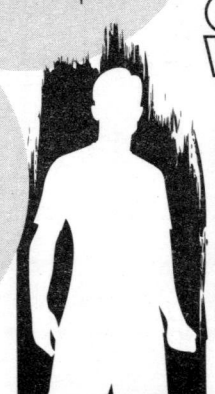

KYLIAN MBAPPÉ

Explosive pace and clinical finishing make this Madrid man one of the most exciting strikers in the world!

REAL MADRID

ARTEM DOVBYK

Artem won the Spanish top-flight's golden boot award in his first season in Spain, before earning a big move to Italy. What a goal machine!

ROMA

OLLIE WATKINS

Pass the ball to Ollie Watkins in any position and he works hard to retain possession and find enough space to create a chance!

ASTON VILLA

CODE BREAKER 2

The manager is changing tactics but doesn't want the opponents to know! Use the code-breaker to work out what the message is!

1 20 20 1 3 11   21 16
20 8 5   18 9 7 8 20
23 9 14 7

CODE BREAKING RULES

Each number represents where the letter comes in the alphabet. For example, 1 is A, 18 is R and 26 is Z.

THE CODED MESSAGE IS:

_ _ _ _ _ _ _ _ _ _ _

_ _ _ _ _ _ _ _ _ _

Answer on page 90.

FRENCH LEAGUE

The French top-flight league might be dominated by a few big clubs, but it's full of great action! How much do you know about it?

DIFFICULTY: ⚽⚽⚽

1 Paris Saint-Germain have won the top-flight league more than any other club. How many times have they won it?

- [ ] 9
- [ ] 12
- [ ] 31
- [ ] 17

2 Which club play home matches at the Stade Pierre-Mauroy?

- [ ] Lille
- [ ] Reims
- [ ] Nantes
- [ ] Monaco

3 How many clubs compete in the league each season?

- [ ] 22
- [ ] 18
- [ ] 20
- [ ] 12

4 Which club has the biggest stadium capacity of 67,394?

- [ ] Rennes
- [ ] Brest
- [ ] Lyon
- [ ] Marseille

5 Who managed Paris Saint-Germain in the 2023-24 season?

- [ ] Luis Enrique
- [ ] Roberto Mancini
- [ ] Patrick Vieira
- [ ] Carlo Ancelotti

6
Which of these players hasn't been the league's top scorer?

- ☑ Edinson Cavani
- ☑ Zlatan Ibrahimović
- ☑ Kylian Mbappé
- ☑ Olivier Giroud

7
Which player scored a hat-trick in 4 minutes and 30 seconds during the 2022-23 season?

- ☑ Marquinhos
- ☑ Elye Wahi
- ☑ Loïs Openda
- ☑ Kylian Mbappé

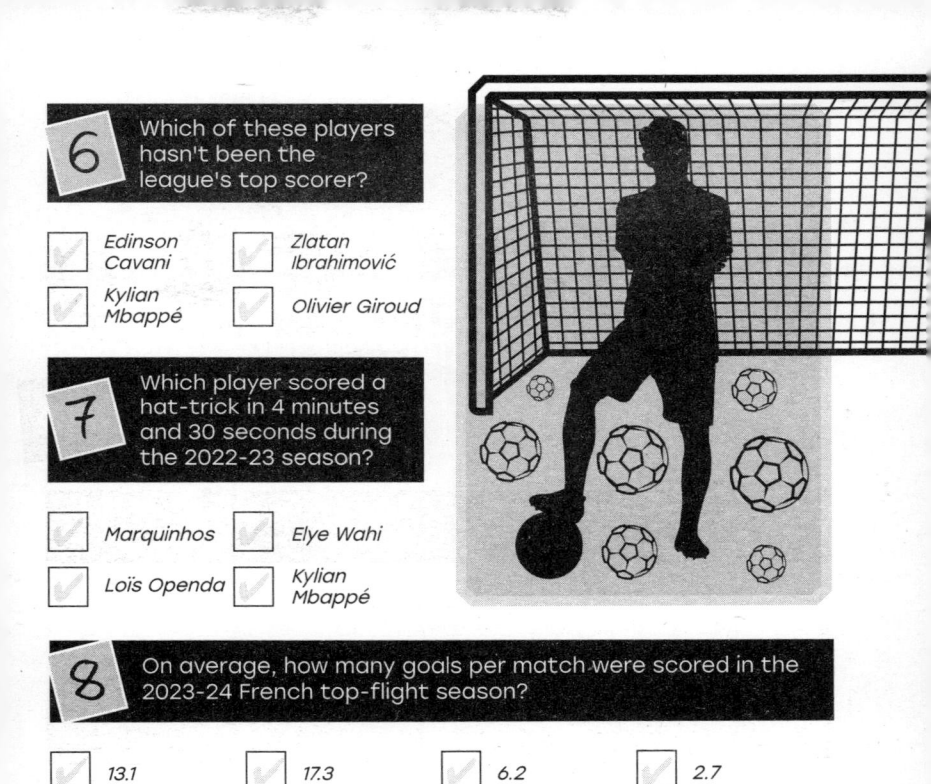

8
On average, how many goals per match were scored in the 2023-24 French top-flight season?

- ☑ 13.1
- ☑ 17.3
- ☑ 6.2
- ☑ 2.7

9
The home shirt of Lens is made up of which two colours?

- ☑ Blue, red
- ☑ Black, blue
- ☑ Yellow, red
- ☑ Grey, white

10
What is the name of the stadium that Nice call home?

- ☑ Allianz Riviera
- ☑ Nice Ground
- ☑ Stadia Nice
- ☑ Very Nice

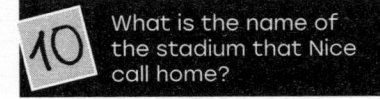

FOOTY FORMATIONS 2

Thought you'd mastered these footy formations? Think again! Draw pictures in the grids so that each column, row and box contains only one of each football symbol.

EASY

TOUGH

WORLD CLASS

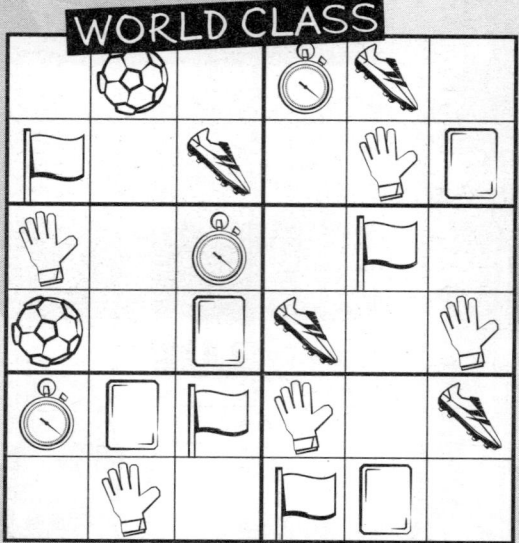

KEY

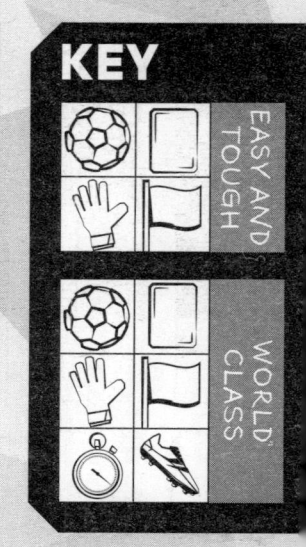

MATCH ATTAX MIX-UP 2

DIFFICULTY:

Another wicked Match Attax card has been divided into six strips. Can you put the card back together and write the correct order the strips need to go in?

A

00 C

B

— 1

C

MATCH ATTAX
TRADING CARD GAME

ASTON VILLA

OLLIE WATKINS

1

DEFENCE
67

D

Topps

FOR

POWER
PLAY
90

9.1M

ATTACK
100

E

KLUB

F

Z

B

 1
 2
 3
 4
 5
 6

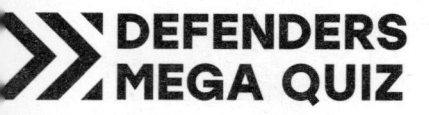

DEFENDERS MEGA QUIZ

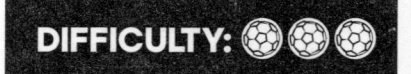

DIFFICULTY:

The last line of defence when the enemy is attacking, their job is simple: stop the ball getting anywhere near the goal. Take this quiz to see if you are a defensive mastermind!

1 Goalscoring defender Cristian Romero plays for which club?

- [ ] Tottenham Hotspur
- [ ] Monaco
- [ ] Real Madrid
- [ ] Celtic

2 What do you call a wide defender that also attacks in wide positions?

- [ ] A bit-lost
- [ ] A wide-ender
- [ ] A defend-long
- [ ] A wing-back

3 In a classic 4-4-2 formation, how many defenders are there?

- [ ] 2
- [ ] 3
- [ ] 4
- [ ] 6

4 Which defender lifted the UEFA Champions League in 2023-24?

- [ ] Crisp
- [ ] Nacho
- [ ] Tortilla
- [ ] Chips

5 Which Rangers player is one of the top-scoring defenders in the world?

- [ ] James Tavernier
- [ ] Kyle Walker
- [ ] Ben Davies
- [ ] Greg Taylor

6 How many own goals did defender Meikayla Moore score in a match between the USA and New Zealand?

- [ ] 1
- [ ] 3
- [ ] 4
- [ ] 5

7 Which national team does Bayern Munich's defensive ace Alphonso Davies represent?

- [ ] USA
- [ ] England
- [ ] Canada
- [ ] Wales

8 Which defender made the most interceptions in the 2023-24 English top-flight league season?

- [ ] Antonee Robinson
- [ ] William Saliba
- [ ] John Stones
- [ ] James Tarkowski

9 Which squad number does legendary defender Virgil van Dijk wear?

- [ ] 6
- [ ] 2
- [ ] 4
- [ ] 21

10 Which defender played more minutes than any other player in the 2023-24 UEFA Champions League?

- [ ] Mats Hummels
- [ ] Antonio Rüdiger
- [ ] Emre Can
- [ ] Ferland Mendy

SCOTTISH LEAGUE

The Scottish top-flight league is full of drama, and is the home of one of the greatest rivalries in the world! How well do you know it?

DIFFICULTY: ⚽ ⚽ ⚽

1 With a capacity of 60,411, what is the biggest stadium in the Scottish top-flight league?

☑ Celtic Park ☑ Easter Road ☑ Rugby Park ☑ Dens Park

2 Which club has won the league for the past three seasons in a row?

☑ Rangers ☑ Kilmarnock
☑ Hearts ☑ Celtic

3 Who play their home fixtures at Pittodrie Stadium?

☑ Dundee Utd ☑ Hibernian
☑ Aberdeen ☑ Motherwell

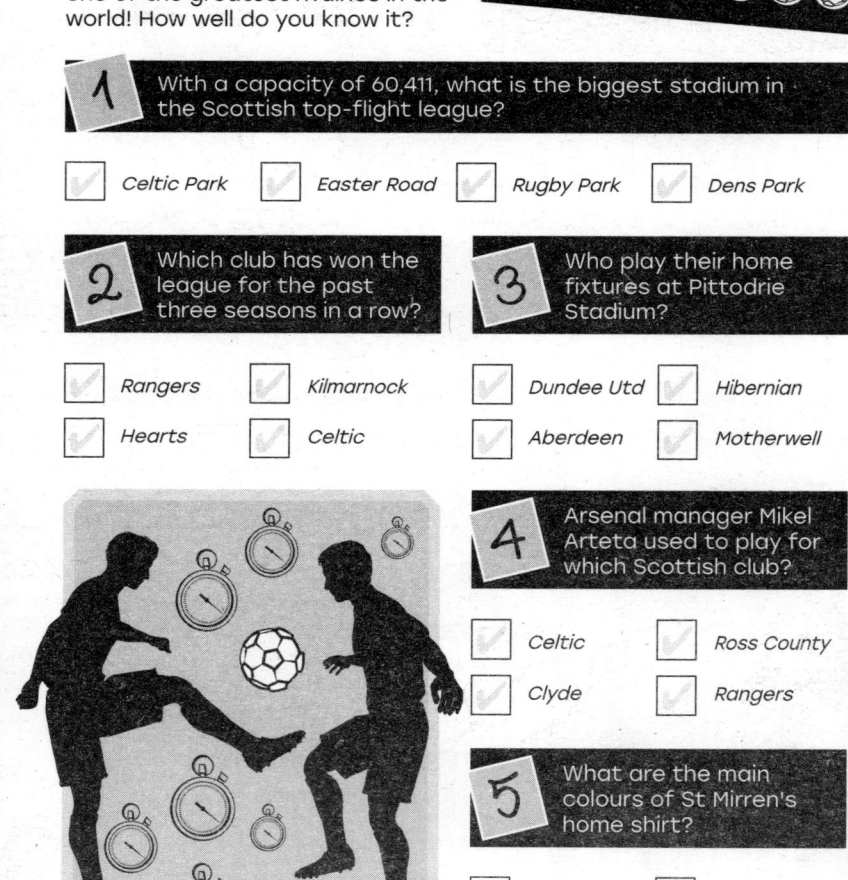

4 Arsenal manager Mikel Arteta used to play for which Scottish club?

☑ Celtic ☑ Ross County
☑ Clyde ☑ Rangers

5 What are the main colours of St Mirren's home shirt?

☑ Red, gold ☑ Blue, Red
☑ Black, white ☑ Blue, silver

6 How long do Scottish top-flight league matches last?

- [ ] 100 mins
- [ ] 80 mins
- [ ] 90 mins
- [ ] 95 mins

7 In their title-winning 2020-21 season, how many matches did Rangers lose?

- [ ] 3
- [ ] 0
- [ ] 1
- [ ] 2

8 How many goals did Lawrence Shankland score for Hearts in the 2023-24 Scottish top-flight season?

- [ ] 19
- [ ] 24
- [ ] 30
- [ ] 12

9 Which two Scottish clubs compete in the Old Firm derby?

- [ ] Celtic, Dundee
- [ ] Rangers, Ross County
- [ ] Rangers, Celtic
- [ ] Aberdeen, Hearts

10 Who is the all-time top scorer in the Scottish top-flight league?

- [ ] Kyogo Furuhashi
- [ ] Lawrence Shankland
- [ ] James Tavernier
- [ ] Kris Boyd

DIFFICULTY:

TRUE ≫ OR ≪ FALSE?

CUP CONUNDRUM!

1
The 2002-03 UEFA Champions League final was won by a score of 8-0!

TRUE ☑

FALSE ☑

2
The last player to be sent off in an English cup final was Mateo Kovačić for Chelsea.

TRUE ☑

FALSE ☑

3
Southampton 'keeper Aaron Ramsdale once conceded five goals in a major cup final.

TRUE ☑

FALSE ☑

4 In a 2022-23 cup final, the referee forgot their kit and had to play in pyjamas!

TRUE ☑

FALSE ☑

5 A 2018 French cup final was played in an empty stadium due to a ticketing error.

TRUE ☑

FALSE ☑

6 Tottenham, Seville and Frankfurt have all played in a UEFA Champions League final ... but never won it.

TRUE ☑

FALSE ☑

7 In the 2023-24 Europa League final, Bayer Leverkusen lost their only match of the entire season.

TRUE ☑

FALSE ☑

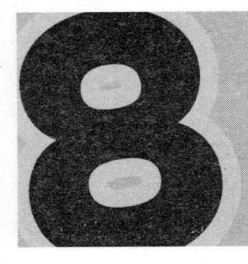

8 Kylian Mbappé has scored more goals in the final of the world's greatest tournament than anyone else.

TRUE ☑

FALSE ☑

Answers on page 92

>> MAGNIFICENT MANAGERS

There's no harder job in football than that of the manager. They choose everything, from the players in the squad to the style of play. Let's look at what makes a great manager!

SKILL 1
TACTICAL IDENTITY

Great managers get their teams playing with a clear identity. From playing deep, pressing or counter-attacking, everyone knows their role!

SKILL 2
RELATIONSHIP MANAGEMENT

Forming a good relationship with trust can give players the confidence to improve. They'll work hard for a manager that shows them respect!

SKILL 3
MAKING CHANGES

Sometimes matches won't go to plan. The best managers can recognise what isn't working and adapt, making changes to tactics or substitutions!

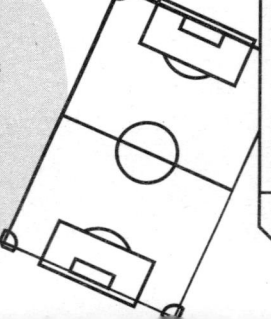

UNAI EMERY

Unai has shown his skills again by taking Aston Villa to the UEFA Champions League in his first season!

ASTON VILLA

CARLO ANCELOTTI

Ancelotti has won it all! It doesn't matter what league he is managing in, Carlo always works out how he can make his team challenge for the title!

REAL MADRID

PEP GUARDIOLA

One of the greatest managers of all time. His teams play with a clear goal and strict discipline, creating chance after chance to score. Legend!

MANCHESTER CITY

TOP SCORERS

We've hidden some of the game's best scorers inside this wordsearch. Time yourself and tick them all off as you find them!

X	R	T	B	E	L	L	I	G	K	J	M	I	A	M
H	B	E	L	L	I	N	G	H	A	M	U	Z	R	C
V	A	S	U	Z	Z	I	R	E	H	W	F	M	M	P
Q	D	A	Q	V	X	F	L	F	C	A	L	J	S	J
J	K	N	L	V	A	X	J	U	M	T	H	W	V	W
I	E	I	R	A	B	X	B	M	B	K	B	W	X	P
N	R	V	L	F	N	N	V	I	A	I	M	N	V	Z
T	R	Y	W	R	O	D	W	I	P	N	U	C	C	G
X	M	Q	E	P	Y	E	H	L	P	S	S	Y	R	J
M	N	R	I	E	V	X	W	Ø	É	Z	Y	I	Q	M
S	H	A	N	K	L	A	N	D	J	V	K	P	U	V
H	P	X	Y	B	Y	S	J	L	D	L	S	A	V	H
T	R	S	A	M	C	E	F	M	B	E	U	N	N	G
G	X	Y	X	B	X	K	W	B	Y	U	C	N	C	E
G	I	U	F	O	D	E	N	A	U	V	C	V	D	P
Z	V	A	Z	Q	Q	D	R	U	S	S	O	D	W	W
X	Y	B	U	U	L	I	R	E	V	P	J	P	I	P

- ☐ Russo
- ☐ Mbappé
- ☐ Kane
- ☐ Watkins
- ☐ Kerr
- ☐ Bellingham
- ☐ Foden
- ☐ Shankland
- ☐ Højlund
- ☐ Haaland

IT TOOK ME...
_____ mins / _____ secs

ITALIAN LEAGUE

Italy is famous for pizza, pasta and some of the most iconic players in the world. How well do you know the Italian top-flight league?

DIFFICULTY:

1 In their title-winning 2023-24 season, what was Inter Milan's longest winning streak of games?

- [ ] 13
- [ ] 11
- [ ] 10
- [ ] 18

2 What is the main colour of the classic Fiorentina home kit?

- [ ] Grey
- [ ] Red
- [ ] Navy blue
- [ ] Purple

3 Who is the captain of 2023-24 season champs, Inter Milan?

- [ ] Lautaro Martínez
- [ ] Paulo Dybala
- [ ] Matías Soulé
- [ ] Federico Chiesa

4 Which team has won the most (36) Italian top-flight league titles?

- [ ] AC Milan
- [ ] Roma
- [ ] Juventus
- [ ] Inter Milan

5 How many clubs compete in the league every season?

- [ ] 22
- [ ] 18
- [ ] 30
- [ ] 20

6 Which club's stadium is named after footy legend Diego Maradona?

- [ ] Juventus
- [ ] Fiorentina
- [ ] Napoli
- [ ] Monza

7 Which of these teams was promoted to the top-flight league for the 2024-25 season?

- [ ] Parma
- [ ] Roma
- [ ] Torino
- [ ] Bologna

8 For how many consecutive seasons have record breakers Inter Milan been in the top-flight league?

- [ ] 103
- [ ] 93
- [ ] 83
- [ ] 23

9 Which team is located the furthest south and on an island?

- [ ] Cagliari
- [ ] Roma
- [ ] Napoli
- [ ] Lazio

10 In the 2023-24 season, who provided the most assists in the league?

- [ ] Marcus Thuram
- [ ] Christian Pulisic
- [ ] Ademola Lookman
- [ ] Paulo Dybala

CLUB LEGENDS 2

DIFFICULTY: ⚽ ⚽

The fans still talk about their on-pitch heroics and the history they made! Can you draw a line between the legends and the clubs they played for?

LEGEND

CLUB

LEGEND	CLUB
ALEXIA PUTELLAS	MANCHESTER CITY
DIDIER DROGBA	CELTIC
SCOTT BROWN	INTER MILAN
DIEGO MARADONA	MANCHESTER UTD
STEPH HOUGHTON	WEST HAM
JAVIER ZANETTI	BARCELONA
PAUL SCHOLES	CHELSEA
JARROD BOWEN	NAPOLI

Answers on page 93

CUP WINNERS

DIFFICULTY:

Start on the top row and work out your route to the bottom by circling the only club on each line that has won a major European trophy!

1	SOUTHAMPTON	GETAFE	MANCHESTER CITY	CELTA VIGO
2	OSASUNA	AC MILAN	LE HAVRE	CRYSTAL PALACE
3	REIMS	LIVERPOOL	BRESTOIS	RENNAIS
4	REAL BETIS	UNION BERLIN	STUTTGART	SEVILLA
5	REAL MADRID	TOULOUSE	ST. MIRREN	ROSS COUNTY
6	HULL	CHELSEA	HOFFENHEIM	RB LEIPZIG

MIDFIELD MEGA QUIZ

Welcome to the team's engine room, where midfielders help out in defence, boss the middle of the park and burst forward into attack. How well do you know the midfielder position?

1. Which club did Jude Bellingham play for before Real Madrid?

- Sunderland
- Borussia Dortmund
- Southampton
- New York City

2. What colour kit are you likely to see Kevin De Bruyne play in?

- Blue
- Purple
- Orange
- Green

3. What nationality is young Barcelona midfielder, Pedri?

- French
- Italian
- Spanish
- Portuguese

4. Which club does mega midfielder Joshua Kimmich play for?

- Arsenal
- Bayern Munich
- Real Madrid
- Sevilla

5 How do you describe a midfielder that sits in front of the defence?

- [ ] Defensive midfielder
- [ ] Forward-back
- [ ] Mid-back
- [ ] Long defender

6 Who is the top-scoring midfielder in English top-flight league history?

- [ ] Mark Noble
- [ ] Frank Lampard
- [ ] Cesc Fàbregas
- [ ] Kevin De Bruyne

7 If a team starts with a 4-3-3 formation, how many midfielders are on the pitch?

- [ ] 2
- [ ] 3
- [ ] 4
- [ ] 0

8 Which midfielder scored the most goals in the English 2023-24 top-flight season?

- [ ] Phil Foden
- [ ] Cole Palmer
- [ ] Declan Rice
- [ ] Eberechi Eze

9 Which squad number does Manchester City's midfield hero, Rodri, wear on his shirt?

- [ ] 21
- [ ] 4
- [ ] 16
- [ ] 24

10 Who made the most assists in the 2023-24 Spanish top-flight season?

- [ ] Pedri
- [ ] Iago Aspas
- [ ] Álex Baena
- [ ] Raphinha

Answers on page 93

SPOT THE DIFFERENCE

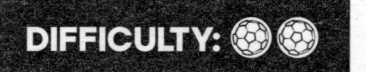

DIFFICULTY: ⚽ ⚽

How sharp is your footballing vision? These two Match Attax cards have eight differences between them. Find and circle all eight when you spot them!

Colour in a football when you find each difference

MISSING DREAM TEAM

The greatest team on Earth has been assembled below, but some of the names are missing letters! Can you fill them in to complete the starting lineup?

_N_NA
GK

WALK__
RB

_IN_S
CB

S_A_
LB

R__E
CM

_O_RI
CM

OWE
RW

GRE_L_SH
LW

S_K_
RF

_AN_
CF

M_A_PÉ
LF

Answers on page 94

WOMEN'S CHAMPIONS LEAGUE

DIFFICULTY: ⚽ ⚽ ⚽

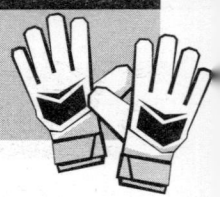

The best of the best clubs in Europe come together to compete in the UEFA Women's Champions League every season! How much of the action can you remember?

1 Which club have won the tournament more than any other?

- [ ] Lyon
- [ ] Arsenal
- [ ] Aston Villa
- [ ] Manchester Utd

2 Who is the top scorer in UEFA Women's Champions League history?

- [ ] Camille Abily
- [ ] Marta
- [ ] Ada Hegerberg
- [ ] Lauren James

3 Which club has Sam Kerr played for since 2020?

- [ ] Manchester City
- [ ] Aston Villa
- [ ] Barcelona
- [ ] Chelsea

4 What colour shirt do Arsenal women's team play in?

- [ ] Red, white
- [ ] Blue, grey
- [ ] Yellow, pink
- [ ] Claret, white

5 Who's made more appearances in the league than anyone else?

- ☑ Mary Earps
- ☑ Sophie Ingle
- ☐ Jordan Nobbs
- ☐ Khadija Shaw

6 Arsenal's Kim Little has scored more penalties than anyone else in the tournament's history. How many?

- ☑ 30
- ☑ 21
- ☑ 19
- ☑ 11

7 What's the capacity of Bayern Munich's home stadium, the FC Bayern Campus?

- ☐ 21,400
- ☑ 2,500
- ☑ 41,000
- ☑ 5,000

8 Which French team play their home matches at the Stade Gérard Houllier?

- ☐ Barcelona
- ☐ Lyon
- ☐ Juventus
- ☐ Roma

9 How many clubs competed in the tournament during the memorable 2023-24 season?

- ☐ 16
- ☑ 20
- ☑ 32
- ☑ 8

10 How many times has Alexia Putellas been the tournament's top scorer?

- ☐ 1
- ☐ 7
- ☐ 3
- ☐ 9

STAT CAN'T BE RIGHT!

Each of these football cards includes player info, but one stat on each card is incorrect. Can you circle the piece of wrong info on each one?

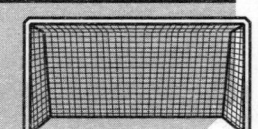

DEKLAN RICE

Team:
Arsenal
Position:
Defensive midfielder
Height:
1.88 m
Born:
1999
Country:
England

AITANA BONMATÍ

Team:
Barcelona
Position:
Defender
Height:
1.61 m
Born:
1998
Country:
Spain

KYLIAN MBAPPÉ

Team:
Real Madrid
Position:
Forward
Height:
1.78 m
Born:
1989
Country:
France

MARCUS THURAM

Team:
AC Milan
Position:
Forward
Height:
1.92 m
Born:
1997
Country:
France

MICHAEL OLISE

Team:
Bayern Munich
Position:
Attacking midfielder
Height:
2.14 m
Born:
2001
Country:
France

MOHAMMED KUDUS

Team:
West Ham
Position:
Goalkeeper
Height:
1.75 m
Born:
2000
Country:
Ghana

ANSWERS!

READY TO SEE HOW YOU'VE DONE?

P8-9

1. False
2. True
3. False
4. True
5. True
6. False
7. False
8. True

P10-11

1. Manuel Neuer
2. Gregor Kobel
3. Lukas Hradecky
4. Petr Čech
5. 2017
6. FC Lorient
7. 18
8. Thomas Kaminski
9. 17
10. 1

P12

1. F
2. A
3. C
4. B
5. E
6. D

P13

D makes it to the goal.

P14

Player 1
Khadija Shaw
Player 2
Ollie Watkins
Player 3
Lauren James
Player 4
Marc-André
ter Stegen

P19

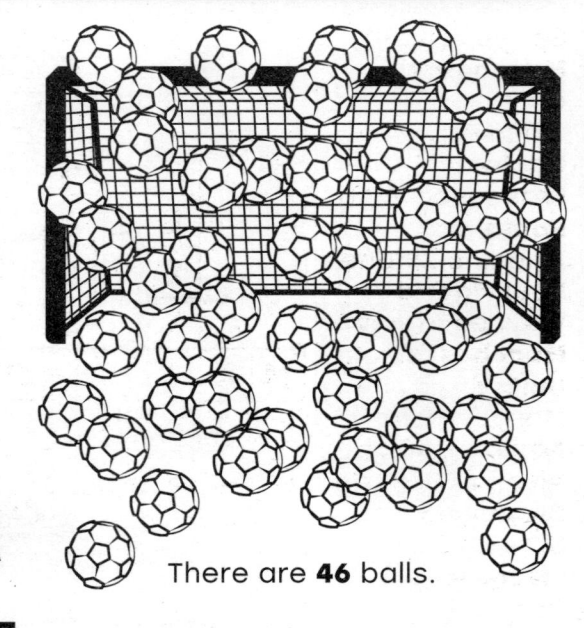

There are **46** balls.

P16-17

1 5
2 5
3 Leicester
4 19
5 English
6 Chelsea
7 0 points. It
was decided
on goal
difference
8 Over 180
9 Arsenal
10 Mary Earps

P20-21

1 Real Madrid
2 Harry Kane,
Kylian Mbappé
3 32
4 Iker Casillas
5 23
6 5
7 4
8 Cristiano
Ronaldo
9 10.1
10 Turf Moor

Sergio Agüero
Manchester City
Sam Kerr
Chelsea
Francesco Totti
Roma
Zinedine Zidane
Real Madrid
Wayne Rooney
Manchester United
Manuel Neuer
Bayern Munich
Aitana Bonmatí
Barcelona
Steven Gerrard
Liverpool

Crossword answers:

1. RODRI
2. ALEXIA
3. NICO
4. RONALD
5. MAINOO
6. VINÍCIUS
7. BOWEN
8. LOOKMAN

P30-31

1 Carlo Ancelotti
2 Arsenal
3 Sir Alex Ferguson
4 Bayer Leverkusen
5 José Mourinho
6 76
7 106
8 Pep Guardiola
9 14
10 Luis Enrique

P24-25

1 Manchester Utd
2 Arsenal
3 Rodri
4 Burnley
5 7
6 Bournemouth
7 5
8 Liverpool
9 Brentford
10 Erling Haaland

P32

Change to the new formation we practiced!

P28-29

1 True
2 False
3 True
4 True
5 False
6 True
7 True
8 False

P33

Player 1
Jude Bellingham
Player 2
Leny Yoro
Player 3
Kylian Mbappé
Player 4
Aitana Bonmatí

P34-35

1. 81,365
2. Gregor Kobel
3. Heidenheim
4. 33
5. Harry Kane
6. RB Leipzig
7. 15
8. 36.41
9. Mainz 05
10. Alejandro Grimaldo

P40

D	M	A	R	T	Í	N	E	Z	J
J	G	W	C	W	Z	I	E	O	I
S	A	J	M	E	M	S	U	L	P
A	V	H	U	I	N	A	Q	G	A
K	I	K	S	C	S	K	M	C	L
A	G	U	I	R	A	S	S	Y	M
Y	A	M	A	L	L	R	Z	F	E
Q	B	J	L	E	I	Q	R	K	R
Q	L	D	A	W	B	F	R	P	O
Z	U	J	V	T	A	C	I	Q	X
Z	X	B	O	W	E	N	S	K	L

P37

Group 1 - 10
Group 2 - 7
Group 3 - 11

P38-39

1. Erling Haaland
2. Darwin Núñez
3. Artem Dovbyk
4. Kylian Mbappé
5. Kadidiatou Diani
6. 24
7. 36
8. Cole Palmer
9. 24
10. Álex Baena

P41	P42

Bayern Munich	Die Roten	**Stadium 1**
Aston Villa	The Villans	Santiago
Manchester City	The Citizens	Bernabéu
RB Leipzig	Die Roten Bullen	**Stadium 2** Anfield
Arsenal	The Gunners	**Stadium 3**
Rangers	The Gers	Celtic Park
Real Madrid	Los Blancos	**Stadium 4**
Manchester United	The Red Devils	Stade Vélodrome

P44-45

1 36
2 Valencia
3 Rayo Vallecano
4 Celta Vigo
5 Camp Nou
6 Árbitro
7 Real Betis
8 Kirian Rodríguez
9 16
10 Lionel Messi

P46

EASY

TOUGH

WORLD CLASS

1 False
2 True
3 False
4 False
5 False
6 False
7 True
8 True

P50-51

P52

1 Wembley
2 105,000
3 1877
4 Cagliari
5 Marseille
6 Athletics
7 Craven Cottage
8 Mallorca
9 Rangers
10 18 (Lazio and Roma share the Stadio Olympico and Inter Milan and AC Milan share the San Siro)

Route C leads to the boots.

P53

Player 1
Mohammed Kudus
Player 2
Patricia Guijarro
Player 3
Alexia Putellas
Player 4
Jude Bellingham

P55

Attack up the right wing

P56-57

1 12
2 Lille
3 18
4 Marseille
5 Luis Enrique
6 Olivier Giroud
7 Loïs Openda
8 2.7
9 Yellow, red
10 Allianz Riviera

EASY

TOUGH

WORLD CLASS

P59

1 C
2 B
3 A
4 E
5 F
6 D

P60-61

1 Tottenham Hotspur
2 A wing-back
3 4
4 Nacho
5 James Tavernier
6 3
7 Canada
8 Antonee Robinson
9 4
10 Mats Hummels

P62-63

1. Celtic Park
2. Celtic
3. Aberdeen
4. Rangers
5. Black, white
6. 90 mins
7. 0
8. 24
9. Rangers, Celtic
10. Kris Boyd

P64-65

1. False
2. True
3. False
4. False
5. False
6. True
7. True
8. True

P67

X	R	T	B	E	L	L	I	G	K	J	M	I	A	M
H	B	E	L	L	I	N	G	H	A	M	U	Z	R	C
V	A	S	U	Z	Z	I	R	E	H	W	F	M	M	P
Q	D	A	Q	V	X	F	L	F	C	A	L	J	S	J
J	K	N	L	V	A	X	J	U	M	T	H	W	V	W
I	E	I	R	A	B	X	B	M	B	K	B	W	X	P
N	R	V	L	F	N	N	V	I	A	I	M	N	V	Z
T	R	Y	W	R	O	D	W	I	P	N	U	C	C	G
X	M	Q	E	P	Y	E	H	L	P	S	S	Y	R	J
M	N	R	I	E	V	X	W	Ø	É	Z	Y	I	Q	M
S	H	A	N	K	L	A	N	D	J	V	K	P	U	V
H	P	X	Y	B	Y	S	J	L	D	L	S	A	V	H
T	R	S	A	M	C	E	F	M	B	E	U	N	N	G
G	X	Y	X	B	X	K	W	B	Y	U	C	N	C	E
G	I	U	F	O	D	E	N	A	U	V	C	V	D	P
Z	V	A	Z	Q	Q	D	R	U	S	S	O	D	W	W
X	Y	B	U	U	L	I	R	E	V	P	J	P	I	P

P68-69

1. 10
2. Purple
3. Lautaro Martínez
4. Juventus
5. 20
6. Napoli
7. Parma
8. 93
9. Cagliari
10. Marcus Thuram

P70

Alexia Putellas
Barcelona
Didier Drogba
Chelsea
Scott Brown
Celtic
Diego Maradona
Napoli
Steph Houghton
Manchester City
Javier Zanetti
Inter Milan
Paul Scholes
Manchester Utd
Jarrod Bowen
West Ham

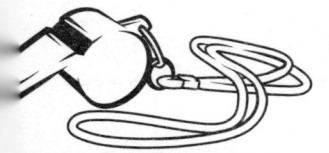

P71

1. Manchester City
2. AC Milan
3. Liverpool
4. Sevilla
5. Real Madrid
6. Chelsea

P72-73

1. Borussia Dortmund
2. Blue
3. Spanish
4. Bayern Munich
5. Defensive midfielder
6. Frank Lampard
7. 3
8. Cole Palmer
9. 16
10. Álex Baena

1. Lyon
2. Ada Hegerberg
3. Chelsea
4. Red, white
5. Sophie Ingle
6. 11
7. 2,500
8. Lyon
9. 16
10. 1

Declan Rice
Name should be Declan

Aitana Bonmatí
Position should be midfielder

Kylian Mbappé
Date of birth should be 1998

Marcus Thuram
Team should be Inter Milan

Michael Olise
Height should be 1.84 m

Mohammed Kudus
Position should be attacking midfielder

GK	Onana	**RW**	Bowen
RB	Walker	**LW**	Grealish
CB	Mings	**RF**	Saka
LB	Shaw	**CF**	Kane
CM	Rice	**LF**	Mbappé
CM	Rodri		

uk.topps.com